I0814285

ESSENTIAL **FITNESS**

HIGH-INTENSITY INTERVAL TRAINING

BY MARIE-THERESE MILLER, PHD

Essential Library

An Imprint of Abdo Publishing
abdobooks.com

ABDOBOOKS.COM
Published by Abdo Publishing, a division of ABDO, PO Box 398166, Minneapolis, Minnesota 55439.

Printed in the United States of America, North Mankato, Minnesota.
052024
092024

Cover Photo: Ivan Dudka/Shutterstock Images
Interior Photos: iStockphoto, 3, 7, 21, 29, 30, 31, 35, 39, 51, 52, 55, 57, 60–61, 72, 76–77, 79, 80, 90–91; Visual Art Agency/iStockphoto, 4–5; Shutterstock Images, 8, 18–19, 36, 42, 48–49, 63, 66, 69, 84, 100–101; Ground Picture/Shutterstock Images, 11; Renata Angerami/iStockphoto, 12; Dikushin Dmitry/Shutterstock Images, 16; Touring Club Italiano/Marka/Universal Images Group/Getty Images, 22; Fly View Productions/iStockphoto, 25, 45, 46; Antonio Diaz/iStockphoto, 32–33, 65, 97; Petri Oeschger/iStockphoto, 40; Ivan Dudka/Shutterstock Images, 59; Dorde Krstic/Shutterstock Images, 64–65; Ivan Pantic/iStockphoto, 74; Hananeko Studio/Shutterstock Images, 83; Max Shutter/Shutterstock Images, 89; Boris Streubel/Getty Images Sport/Getty Images, 93; Shurkin Son/Shutterstock Images, 95; Monkey Business Images/Shutterstock Images, 98; Nando Martinez/iStockphoto, 101

Editor: Charlie Beattie
Series Designer: Jake Slavik

Library of Congress Control Number: 2023949592

PUBLISHER'S CATALOGING-IN-PUBLICATION DATA
Names: Miller, Marie-Therese, author.
Title: High-intensity interval training / by Marie-Therese Miller
Description: Minneapolis, Minnesota: Abdo Publishing, 2025 | Series: Essential fitness | Includes online resources and index.
Identifiers: ISBN 9781098293284 (lib. bdg.) | ISBN 9798384912552 (ebook)
Subjects: LCSH: Physical fitness--Juvenile literature. | Interval training--Juvenile literature. | HIIT (High-intensity interval training)--Juvenile literature. | Muscles--Juvenile literature. | Exercise--Juvenile literature.
Classification: DDC 613.71--dc23

CONTENTS

CHAPTER

HITTING A WALL

As soon as Bret hit his forehand, he knew he was in trouble. Bret's shot was short. As it landed near the service line, his opponent was charging in, ready to unleash a mighty return. Bret knew immediately he would have to get across the court to try and cut off the angle.

Bret's legs felt like they were made of lead. He tried to move, but it seemed like slow motion. By the time he reached the right spot, the ball was whizzing past his outstretched racket.

Bret stood for a second with his hands on his knees, trying to catch his breath. He thought to himself, *How did this happen?* Bret wiped his sweat-drenched forehead with his sleeve. Then he trudged back to the baseline to wait for the next serve.

Sports such as tennis, with periods of intense activity followed by rests, mirror high-intensity interval training.

Coach Cline was watching from the stands. He could tell his star player was completely out of gas. Before the season, Coach Cline had suggested that Bret try high-intensity interval training (HIIT). He thought it might help Bret feel more fit for these tougher matches.

Bret had mentioned that between a packed schedule of school, homework, and practice, he didn't feel he had the time for extra workouts. As Coach Cline watched Bret struggle through the third set, he made a note to bring up the subject again.

HIIT AND SPORTS

HIIT is beneficial for sports such as hockey, football, rugby, and tennis that feature alternating periods of intense activity and rest. However, HIIT can aid other sports training as well. "Performance in the more classical endurance-based events such as the 10k run or distance swimming can [be] improved by incorporating higher intensity interval training even if [it is] at the expense of some volume," says fitness coach Jacky Anderson.[1]

COURT TIME

As long as he could remember, all Bret wanted to do was play tennis. His dad bought him his first racket when Bret was five. Soon, Bret was begging his parents to go to the park every day and hit with him. When they got tired, Bret would stay on the court, smacking shot after shot off the practice wall.

HIIT workouts can help build endurance, which makes them ideal for sports training.

It wasn't long before his parents couldn't keep up. But Bret never stopped wanting to play. He went to the park after school every day with friends to get in a quick set or two before dinner. If no one else was around, he could practice his serves. And there was always the wall.

When the weather got cold, he went to the indoor tennis center and played as long as he could. He even

HIIT workouts can be done without equipment, but they can also involve weights, such as kettlebells.

got a part-time job cleaning the locker rooms when he found out that employees could play for free. His boss, Mr. Turner, had never seen someone so obsessed with the sport. He started calling Bret "Pete" after the legendary champion Pete Sampras.

All that time had paid off. Coach Cline had named Bret the top singles player by his junior season. That meant Bret would be matching up with the No. 1 singles player from every other school. He was excited and a little nervous. Late in the winter he had slipped on an icy sidewalk and sprained his knee. Luckily the injury wasn't severe, but the doctors had told Bret to rest for six weeks.

For once, he had to stay off the court. He worried he would be rusty when he got back to playing, just in time for the spring season. But he'd still managed to impress Coach Cline and win the top singles spot.

DEAD LEGS

Now, in the first match of the season, it was all going wrong. The first set had been a breeze. Bret's shots were crisp. He was exploding into his serves, and his opponent was having trouble returning them. Bret cruised to a 6–1 victory.

The second set of the match was a different story. About halfway through, Bret noticed he was losing his sharpness. Shots that he normally put right down the line had started to drift wide. The two players were tied 4–4, but Bret lost the next two games, and with them, the set.

Now, in the deciding set, nothing was going right. Bret couldn't get a shot to fall inside the lines. And when he thought about going to the net, it seemed like it was miles away. With every point, he grew more and more frustrated.

Meanwhile, his opponent only seemed to get better. Serves whizzed past Bret for aces. And whenever Bret did manage to drop in a good shot, the other player seemed like he was always in the right place. Before Bret knew it, the third set was over. He had lost the match.

AN EXERCISE BUDDY

Exercising with a friend can make the workout more social and more enjoyable. A little friendly competition might even push someone to work out harder. In addition, friends can encourage each other to exercise regularly. If one friend is reluctant to exercise on a certain day, the other can keep them accountable. A person is more likely to work out when a friend is relying on them.

A NEW PLAN

The next day, Bret stopped by Coach Cline's history classroom during his free period. Coach Cline had always been a great mentor. Bret hoped he would have some answers.

"That was a tough one yesterday," Coach Cline said. "How are you feeling?"

"I don't get it. I'm still exhausted today," Bret replied. "I'm not sure what happened. I just lost it there."

"That's what happens when we get tired," said Coach Cline. "Do you feel like you're in good shape?"

If Coach Cline had asked him that question the day before, Bret's answer would have been a definite yes. But now he realized that the time off from his sprained knee might have slowed him down more than he thought.

HIIT workouts can often be done at home.

Having a partner to exercise with can provide extra support and motivation.

Bret had never felt like he needed much exercise. Playing tennis every day had kept him active and in good shape. Or at least that's what he assumed.

"You know, I've never been able to fit in an exercise routine," Bret said. "I kind of thought just playing tennis would take care of that for me."

Coach Cline smiled. "As the competition gets better, you have to work harder," he said. "But I think I have just the thing for you."

"Is it more hours in the day?" Bret joked.

"You don't need more time," said Coach Cline. "You just have to get more efficient."

Coach Cline mentioned HIIT again, saying he thought it would fit perfectly into Bret's busy day. "There's 45 minutes between the end of school and the start of practice each day," Coach Cline said. "Meet me at the courts, and we'll make the most of it. I'll join you. I could use some work myself."

The next day, Bret raced out after the final bell. Coach Cline was waiting. They started with a light warm-up by jogging four times around the courts. Then they did four sets of burpees. By the end of the fourth set, Bret could barely jump off the ground.

"Man, I thought my legs were strong!" he said.

"You're doing great," Coach Cline replied. "On to the next one!"

The next one was a plank, but with a twist. Bret had to keep alternating bringing each arm to touch the opposite shoulder. They did those four times for one minute each, resting for 90 seconds in between. Bret now felt tired through his shoulders and chest, as well as his legs. But they weren't even close to finished yet.

The next move was a round of squat jumps. Bret tried to explode out of the squat position each time. As he moved through the sets, he felt his quads burning and the jumps got shorter and shorter. He was exhausted, but there were still three exercises left. Bret could see why the term *high-intensity* was in this workout's name.

Coach Cline put them through a round of four 30-second sprints. Even though Bret's legs and lungs were burning, he made sure he kept pushing himself as hard as he could. Coach Cline kept reminding him that the key to HIIT was to go all-out on every exercise and try to recover as best he could during the brief recovery periods. That would push his heart rate up to the levels that made HIIT effective.

When they did mountain climbers, Bret felt exhausted. But each time he was ready to give up, he remembered that horrible first match. That gave him the motivation to keep driving his knees forward until the timer was up.

They finished the workout with a round of high knees. By the time they were finished, both Bret and Coach Cline were doubled over, trying to catch their breath. Coach Cline had just enough energy to raise one arm up for a fist bump. "Awesome job," he said. "Are you ready for practice?"

WHAT TIME IS BEST?

For years, researchers have been trying to determine the best time of day to exercise. There has never been a conclusive finding. But many who study fitness and exercise say that the time of day a person works out isn't as important as regularity overall. "People who exercise consistently see better fitness results in the long term," write fitness and nutrition experts Amanda Capritto and Giselle Castro-Sloboda.[2]

BURPEES FOR BREAKFAST

Bret and Coach Cline met twice each week to run through different HIIT workouts. Bret even started to enjoy them. He began reading about the benefits of HIIT. He wished he could do them more often, but from his research he found out that overtraining wasn't healthy and could cause injuries, so he made sure he stuck to doing HIIT workouts just two days per week.

On the court, Bret started to feel the effects. His legs felt more explosive. And as the matches got longer, he found himself able to perform just as well at the end of the match as he did in the first few points. By the time Bret had won four matches in a row, his nightmare first day was a distant memory.

Burpees work several parts of the body, including the legs, arms, and abdominals.

After a month of working out with Coach Cline, Bret decided he was ready to change things up. He told his coach that he'd like to move his workouts to the mornings. As much as the exercise was helping, he did like having a few minutes after school to see his friends, relax, and simply be a kid. But Bret figured that if he got up a half-hour earlier each day, he could squeeze in a quick, productive workout before he got to school. That way he could keep his momentum without disrupting the rest of his schedule.

"Well, I'll miss having you as a workout partner, but I think it's a great idea," said Coach Cline. "You've done a great job. I'm proud of you for taking the leap!"

Bret assured his coach that he wouldn't miss a workout. And sure enough, he didn't. Twice per week he got up, had a light snack, and got to work. Each day before practice, Coach Cline would start with one question. "What did you have for breakfast, Bret?"

"Burpees, Coach."

As the weeks went on, Bret continued to dominate matches. In the rare event that someone pushed him to a third set, Bret was no longer worried about running out of gas. Now every opponent he faced was struggling to keep up with him.

WHAT IS HIGH-INTENSITY INTERVAL TRAINING?

HIIT is an exercise program that alternates periods of high-intensity exercise with less demanding periods of exercise or passive rest. HIIT begins with a warm-up. Then there is a period of energetic or intense movements. During this intense section, known as a work period, the person's heart rate rises close to its maximum.

The intervals of less vigorous exercise or passive rest are called recovery periods. The heart rate slows during these intervals. This exercise feels more comfortable and is easier to perform. A HIIT workout finishes with a cooldown.

HIIT is one of the most popular workout modes in the United States.

The amounts of time spent in the work periods and recovery periods differ depending on the workout chosen. The time for each work period may be as short as five seconds or as long as eight minutes. Often, people choose a one-to-one ratio for work and recovery periods. For example, a person might sprint for two minutes, then do a light jog for two minutes. These intervals can be adjusted to the person's fitness level and goals. And the entire workout can be completed in just 20 or 30 minutes.

The warm-up before a HIIT workout usually lasts about five minutes. The warm-up involves low-intensity exercises. It prepares the body for the hard workout ahead. A warm-up safely and slowly raises the heart rate and breathing rate. It raises the body temperature and provides blood to the muscles. Warming up lessens the chance of injury during a workout.

A cooldown after a HIIT workout may take about ten minutes. Like the warm-up, it involves lower intensity exercise followed by stretches. The cooldown allows the heart rate and breathing to gradually slow and return to pre-exercise levels. The blood that has been pumped to the large muscles can return to the heart. Without a cooldown, the blood can pool in the large muscles, stopping it from reaching the brain and causing a person to feel dizzy or faint. A proper cooldown prevents issues such as these.

Warming up with a foam roller or bands is a great way to prepare for HIIT workouts.

THE HISTORY OF HIIT

HIIT dates back to athletic training in the 1930s. During that decade, Swedish coach Gösta Holmér and German coach Woldemar Gerschler designed interval training for elite athletes. Olympic gold-medal runner Emil Zátopek made this style of training more widely known in the 1950s. Since then, high-intensity workouts that involve intervals of all-out effort have often been used to train Olympic athletes. The technique is sometimes called sprint interval training.

In 1996, Japanese exercise scientist Izumi Tabata studied a very demanding high-intensity intermittent training program. It now bears his name. Tabata's method uses the term *intermittent* instead of *interval* because after 20 seconds of maximum effort, the person stops completely for a ten-second rest. Tabata's training was originally designed for use on stationary bicycles. A Tabata workout today follows the same technique using many types of exercises.

Emil Zátopek won three gold medals at the 1952 Olympics in Helsinki, Finland.

WHY IS HIIT SO POPULAR?

HIIT has become a popular workout format. One major reason is that it can be done in much less time than other exercise routines, such as moderate-intensity continuous training (MICT). MICT involves aerobic exercise that is done at a moderate intensity, about 65 to 75 percent of a person's maximum heart rate, for the entire workout.[1] The suggested time for a MICT workout is 60 minutes.[2] On the other hand, a HIIT session can be completed in roughly half the time.

Studies have shown that HIIT provides equal or better health benefits when compared with MICT. Often people are discouraged by the amount of time they need to set aside in their busy schedules for regular exercise. With HIIT, they need to carve out only about a half hour to get a solid workout.

AEROBIC AND ANAEROBIC

Exercise can use aerobic or anaerobic metabolism. Aerobic means that the skeletal muscle cells are using oxygen to provide energy for contraction. Aerobic exercises include dancing, swimming, and walking. Anaerobic exercise is a burst of intense exercise that exceeds the cellular capacity to use oxygen, meaning the skeletal muscles must get energy from other sources. Weight lifting and sprinting are examples of exercises that rely on the anaerobic system. HIIT can involve both aerobic and anaerobic exercise.

Another appealing aspect of HIIT is that it provides many

WHAT TO WEAR

For HIIT, a person should choose clothing that is comfortable and allows for free movement. The fabric should be moisture wicking, which means it does not absorb sweat and allows sweat to move away from the body. In addition, fabrics should be breathable, which means they let air flow through them. Cotton is not a great choice because it absorbs water. Some recommended materials are polyester, nylon, and bamboo fabric.

options. A wide variety of exercises can make up a HIIT routine, so a person can choose the exercises they like. For example, someone might choose running, walking, swimming, dancing, rowing, or any other type of exercise.

It is important for a person to pick an exercise that they enjoy. This will make them more likely to stick with the exercise program, keeping up a habit of exercising on a regular basis over time. The flexibility of HIIT also means that people can change their workout for variety. They might run one day and row another. This variety helps to keep things fresh.

HIIT is also low cost and accessible. It doesn't require an expensive gym membership or specific equipment. People can simply bike or walk around their neighborhood. They might dance in their living room. Exercises that use body weight, such as squats, push-ups, and lunges, can be performed as part of a HIIT workout. People can wear comfortable clothes made of breathable material, along with supportive shoes.

Rowing machines are one of the many machines exercisers can use to build endurance and gain strength through HIIT workouts.

While HIIT can be done at home, going to a gym may open up more options. Specialized workout equipment offers a wider variety of aerobic exercises to incorporate. People can do a HIIT workout using rowing machines, elliptical machines, treadmills, or stationary bikes.

Before people begin a new exercise program, they should consult a doctor or other medical professional. They should make sure they don't have any medical problems that could get worse or pose a danger during exercise. A medical professional can give guidance about whether HIIT is a good fit for an individual. Due to the high intensity and the need for rest, experts agree that HIIT workouts shouldn't be done on two days in a row.

DETERMINING EXERCISE INTENSITY

HIIT exercises elevate a person's heart rate to various levels, depending on how hard they are pushing. There is no universal standard for determining a person's maximum heart rate, but a few different formulas are commonly used. In one, a person can subtract their age from 220. For example, a 20-year-old's maximum rate would be 200 beats per minute.[3] That number would be the highest number of beats per minute the person would strive to reach in a workout.

In another formula, the person multiplies their age by 0.7, then subtracts that number from 208. For example, if the person is 20, multiplying their age by 0.7 gives them 14. Subtracting from 208 gives them a maximum heart rate of 194 beats per minute.[4]

People planning HIIT workouts should determine their heart rate goals for both the work period and recovery period. A person may wish to get close to their maximum heart rate during the work period and keep their heart rate at half that amount during the recovery period. To keep track of heart rate during a workout, people often use smart watches or dedicated heart rate monitors.

However, someone without such a device can find their heart rate by feeling their pulse on their wrist or neck. They hold two fingers to either spot and count the number of beats they feel in a minute. They can also hold for only 15 seconds, and then multiply their count by four.[5]

There are other ways to determine exercise intensity besides heart rate. One study showed that people can accurately determine how intensely they are exercising. Swedish researcher Gunnar Borg devised a scale that rates perceived exertion from six to 20, with six meaning no exertion at all and 20 being maximal exertion. Borg also found that these numbers were aligned with a person's heart rate when they were multiplied by 10. If a person reported an exertion level of 12, or

KEEPING FEET SAFE

People doing HIIT in a specific sport should use the footwear recommended for that sport. For example, runners should wear running shoes, which are designed for the motion of that activity. For court sports, such as basketball, the person should use a shoe designed to protect against ankle sprains. It is also important to get the proper fit for the shoe. The toes should have room to move. There should be a thumb's width of room between the largest toe and the end of the shoe. The heel should not slip up and down.

moderate intensity, their heart rate would be around 120 beats per minute.[6]

Scientists tested the scale by measuring participants' heart rates. They also tested each person's oxygen consumption to determine the subject's VO2 max, which calculates a person's maximum amount of oxygen used during full-effort exercise. The researchers compared the measurements to the subjects' self-reported levels of exertion on Borg's scale. They found that the subjects were reliable in their perceptions. In other words, they could accurately feel how hard they were exercising.

Another way to determine exercise intensity is through the talk test. When exercising at an intense level during HIIT, it should be difficult to carry on a conversation. During the moderate-intensity recovery period, talking should be easier. However they are calculated, it is important for exercisers to know their levels of exertion. That way they will know when to push harder or when to back off.

HIIT workouts can be very tiring despite taking far less time than traditional exercise forms.

TRACKING HEART RATE

Technology can help when it comes to exercise. Wearable fitness trackers or watches offer many options to inspire and track workouts. For HIIT, these technologies can be used to monitor heart rate. This will help keep the person within the proper heart rate range during the working and recovery periods. Devices can also monitor interval times so the person knows when to switch from work to recovery period and back again.

There are many different types of fitness trackers available. Many people opt to simply use their smartphone as a fitness tracking device, either through a pre-installed program or a downloaded app. Other types of trackers are wearable devices. Many are worn on the forearm or wrist.

Phones and wristbands are popular ways to track fitness goals.

These trackers come with light-emitting diodes (LEDs) that illuminate the blood vessels underneath the skin and allow sensors to measure heart rate.

The most accurate sensors are bands that are strapped around the chest while exercising. The bands use built-in electrode sensors to detect the heartbeat. That data is then sent to another device, such as a watch or smartphone. Because the bands need an electrical signal to function, they need to be wet while they are being used. This requires either water or sometimes a special gel that comes with the device.

CHAPTER

HIGH-INTENSITY INTERVAL TRAINING AND THE BODY

HIIT is proven to have many benefits for the body. It improves cardiovascular health to keep the heart and blood vessels healthy. The respiratory benefits of HIIT promote healthy lungs.

HIIT also strengthens bones and muscles. It makes the body better at generating energy, and it can lower the risk of certain diseases. In addition to physical benefits, HIIT can also aid mental health.

HIIT AND A HEALTHY HEART

It is important to have a healthy heart. Studies show that HIIT can help keep the heart strong.

HIIT workouts keep a person's heart rate elevated for extended periods of time.

HEARTFELT EXERCISE

In her article "High-Intensity Exercise and Your Heart," medical writer Julie Corliss explains, "The main advantage to HIIT is that you can boost your cardiovascular fitness faster by working harder instead of longer." However, Corliss goes on to explain that HIIT may not be for everyone. She quotes her colleague I-Min Lee as saying, "HIIT is a great regimen for people who are young and healthy. If you're older or have heart disease, check with your doctor before trying it."[1]

The heart is an organ made of muscle. When it pumps blood through the body, the blood brings oxygen and nutrients to the body, and it removes carbon dioxide and waste products.

Many studies link HIIT to stronger hearts that pump blood more efficiently. Researchers have found that HIIT increases the heart's peak stroke volume, cardiac output, and heart rate. Stroke volume is how much blood the heart sends out to the body with each heartbeat. Cardiac output is how much blood the heart pumps in a minute. The same researchers also found indications that HIIT is likely to be more effective at achieving these increases than moderate-intensity exercise.

Studies have also shown that HIIT can lower blood pressure. Blood pressure is the force that blood exerts against the walls of blood vessels. High blood pressure, or hypertension, can cause many health problems. If a person's blood pressure is too high, their heart is working too hard to pump their blood. This can lead to heart attacks and strokes. High blood pressure can also cause damage to blood vessels.

In one study, researchers tested 28 men between the ages of 18 and 45. The researchers had the men do HIIT exercises on stationary bikes three times per week for six weeks. The results showed that this training was effective in reducing the participants' blood pressure.

HIIT helps keep blood vessels healthy, too. Elastic, flexible blood vessels circulate blood more easily. Vessels that become stiff are linked to cardiovascular disease, kidney disease, and impaired cognition.

Many gyms offer HIIT-style classes.

People often report feeling a boost in stamina after a period of HIIT exercises.

In addition, research has shown that HIIT can combat age-related stiffening of the blood vessels. In one experiment, Gustavo de Oliveira and his fellow researchers studied 25 young women. One group of women did HIIT, and the other did MICT. The researchers found that after eight weeks of exercise, both HIIT and MICT workouts reduced arterial stiffening in participants.

BETTER BREATHING

The lungs work by taking in oxygen for the body to use. This oxygen supply enters red blood cells and is then pumped throughout the body by the heart. Carbon dioxide, which is the waste product of these cells, travels through the blood back to the lungs, where it is exhaled.

Because of this process, it is vital for the lungs to be healthy in order to keep cells supplied with oxygen.

HIIT can improve lung function and increase VO2 max. Researchers studied 15 people who did four weeks of HIIT. They found that even in this relatively short time, the participants showed an increase in VO2 max. HIIT also strengthened the muscles that power the lungs.

HIIT can even improve the lungs of those with chronic obstructive pulmonary disease (COPD). COPD is a condition that makes it difficult to breathe. It gets worse over time. Emphysema is a form of COPD. With emphysema, the walls of the lungs' air sacs are damaged. Chronic bronchitis, another type of COPD, creates both excess inflammation and mucus in a person's airways. Research has shown that HIIT can improve lung function and lung capacity in people with COPD.

STRONG BONES

HIIT can make bones stronger. They protect internal organs, such as the heart and lungs. Bones are made of collagen and calcium, which makes them flexible and strong.

Nutrition, including getting plenty of calcium and vitamin D, is important to promote bone growth and bone density. Another way to keep bones strong is to exercise consistently. Weight-bearing exercises are recommended for bone strength. These exercises involve the body moving against gravity. HIIT can incorporate many kinds of weight-bearing exercises, such as dancing or jogging.

POWERFUL MUSCLES

The muscles in a person's body serve several functions. Skeletal muscles are attached to bones for protection. They keep a person's posture straight and provide heat and fuel for the body.

When a person's body moves, it is as a result of these muscles contracting. Every movement, from something as simple as a smile to more complex motions such as running or swimming, involves muscle contractions. Nerves in these muscles receive signals from the brain with instructions on not only what to move but how quickly and forcefully.

HIIT increases muscle power. Muscle power is used when a person needs muscles to be forceful in short, fast bursts. In one experiment, researchers studied as 13 triathletes participated in five weeks of HIIT. At the end, the researchers tested the athletes' ability to jump vertically. They found that HIIT improved vertical jumping height.

In another experiment, researchers studied 33 sedentary men between the ages of 56 and 65.

They found that six weeks of HIIT increased the participants' muscle power. Muscle power is one of the most important factors in protecting older people from injuries due to falls.

METABOLISM AND ENERGY

Metabolism is the way the body transfers its energy from the food and drink ingested. This process takes place in

HIIT workouts are excellent for building muscle.

Despite featuring short bursts of exercise, HIIT workouts can be effective training for distance runners.

the body's cells. Parts inside the cells called mitochondria use oxygen, fat, glucose, and amino acids from the blood and muscle to make adenosine triphosphate (ATP). ATP is chemical energy that the body's cells can use.

Muscles have many mitochondria because muscles need lots of energy to keep moving. With consistent exercise, the muscles will make more mitochondria so they can keep up with the new energy demands. HIIT stimulates the muscles to make more mitochondria.

In addition, HIIT can help the existing mitochondria work more effectively. Mayo Clinic researchers studied 72 sedentary adults. After 12 weeks of HIIT, they found that the younger people in the group, between 18 and 30 years old, showed a 49 percent increase in mitochondrial capacity. The cells were better able to take in oxygen and produce energy. The mitochondrial growth was even more pronounced for older members of the study. People between 65 and 80 years old showed a 69 percent increase in mitochondrial capacity.[2]

LOWERING CANCER RISK

Exercise, including HIIT, might help to lower the risk of particular types of cancers. Cancer is a disease in which the body's cells grow out of control. Forty percent of people in the United States will be diagnosed with cancer during their lifetime.[3]

The National Cancer Institute says that there are several reasons that exercise might reduce cancer risks. Exercise can result in lower levels of hormones that are

BURNING CALORIES

Calories are the fuel inside the body that is burned during everyday activities. HIIT burns many calories in a short period of time. This doesn't end when the workout is over. People who exercise using HIIT experience excess post-exercise oxygen consumption (EPOC), also known as afterburn. This means that the body keeps using energy and burning calories after the exercise period is over. EPOC after HIIT can last several hours.

linked to certain cancers. Exercise reduces inflammation and improves the immune system, which helps lower cancer risk. In addition, exercise speeds digestion and more quickly takes cancer-causing substances out of the digestive system.

One study looked at an everyday version of HIIT and its link to lower cancer risk. Emmanuel Stamatakis and his colleagues studied 22,000 non-exercisers. The subjects were given devices to track their daily activities. They found that only 4.5 minutes of vigorous activity each day reduces cancer risk by up to 32 percent when compared

Many gyms are equipped with battle ropes, which can be a very demanding HIIT workout.

with those who continued to avoid exercising.[4]

The researchers called it vigorous intermittent lifestyle physical activity (VILPA). VILPA consists of short intense periods of exercise throughout the day. VILPA might include a speed walk or a quick, vigorous run. Stamatakis says, "VILPA is a bit like applying high-intensity interval training (HIIT) to your everyday life."[5]

One study linked HIIT with the slowing of certain cancers. Researchers studied 52 men with prostate cancer. They had the men do 12 weeks of HIIT workouts. At the end of that time, the researchers discovered that the prostate cancer cell growth slowed in the participants.

HIGH-INTENSITY EXERCISE AND METASTATIC CANCER

Metastatic cancer is cancer that spreads from where it began to another area of the body. Carmit Levy and fellow researchers at Tel Aviv University in Israel followed 2,734 Israeli men and women for 20 years. In that time, 234 of the subjects were diagnosed with some form of cancer. Levy's team then observed that those 234 people were 72 percent less likely to develop metastatic cancer if they regularly engaged in high-intensity aerobic exercise.[6] The researchers observed an increased absorption of sugar into internal organs during intense aerobic exercise. In this way, the organs were taking the fuel, so the cancer didn't get the fuel it needed for growth.

MENTAL HEALTH

HIIT can help improve mental health as well as physical health. It has been linked to improved mental well-being in people with depression. People with depression may have feelings of sadness or emptiness that won't go away. They might not feel good about themselves. They often do not find joy in things they used to enjoy. They can feel very tired. Lifestyle changes, such as improved diet and better sleep, can help lessen these symptoms.

Exercise has also been linked to improvement of depressive symptoms. When a person does high-intensity exercise, hormones known as endorphins get released by the brain. These chemicals lift the person's mood, providing some relief. Michael Craig Miller, a faculty member of Harvard Medical School, writes, "For some people [exercise] works as well as antidepressants, although exercise alone isn't enough for someone with severe depression."[7]

Researchers found HIIT effective in reducing the severity of depressive symptoms. They noted that the greater improvement in symptoms occurs when HIIT workouts are performed regularly for at least seven weeks. They concluded that HIIT is an effective method of improving mental health. HIIT was found to be as effective as MICT in this benefit. The fact that HIIT can be done quickly may be a good motivator for people with depression to stick with HIIT.

HIIT can also lessen the symptoms of anxiety. Anxiety is a mental disorder that comes in many forms.

Exercising can improve mood by releasing endorphins or by simply refocusing the mind.

Some anxiety sufferers might worry often. Because of this, they may feel on edge or jittery. People with generalized anxiety disorder can feel tired. It can also affect cognitive functions, making it hard to concentrate. Another type of anxiety is called panic disorder. The fear that people with panic disorder experience comes in sudden intense episodes known as panic attacks.

Many studies have also found that HIIT is helpful in reducing the symptoms of various anxiety disorders. One study involved 33 patients with generalized

HIIT workouts should always be tailored to specific workout goals, especially for those new to exercise or recovering from an injury.

anxiety disorder. Some patients did HIIT workouts, and others did low-intensity workouts. The researchers found that HIIT was twice as effective in reducing anxiety symptoms.[9] HIIT specifically reduced worrying and the physical symptoms associated with anxiety. In a study of patients with panic disorder, 12 participants did 12 weeks of HIIT. The researchers found that HIIT reduced the severity of the panic disorder symptoms.

HIIT can be effective in reducing anxiety, but researchers note that those with anxiety may want to use a longer recovery period between sets and between workouts. This is because anxiety's physical symptoms are similar to the body's response to high-intensity exercise. Both high-intensity exercise and anxiety produce sweating and a fast heart rate. Longer recovery periods and more frequent rest days can prevent these factors from leading to additional anxiety.

BODY-WEIGHT HIIT

While all forms of HIIT have the advantage of being brief, efficient workouts, body-weight HIIT carries an extra advantage. Since they require little to no equipment, body-weight HIIT exercises can be done virtually anywhere. That makes them an excellent option for those without access to a gym, who are traveling, or who have limited space at home.

Body-weight exercises are exercise movements where a person's primary form of resistance comes from their own weight. Something as simple as a push-up or sit-up is a body-weight movement. And those types of movements can be done at various rates of intensity, including as part of a HIIT workout.

Body-weight HIIT workouts take simple exercise movements and perform them at greater intensities.

QUICK WORKOUT, BIG RESULTS

When HIIT principles are combined with body-weight exercise, the result can be a highly effective workout. A study carried out by 11 exercise scientists from the United States, Canada, and Brazil analyzed 12 adults, including six men and six women. On one day, the participants sprinted on a treadmill for 60-second intervals, followed by a rest period. The next day, the same participants performed body-weight HIIT exercises at full effort for the same amount of time.

The study looked at multiple fitness metrics, including percentage of VO2 max and heart rates. The participants' blood lactate levels were also measured. This is the amount of lactate in the bloodstream, which indicates the usage of anaerobic metabolism. The higher the lactate level, the greater the amount of muscle fatigue. While the percentage of VO2 max and heart rate measurements were slightly higher when sprinting on a treadmill, the blood lactate levels were higher when

DON'T OVERDO IT

While HIIT has many benefits, experts warn people not to do HIIT too often. One study showed that people who performed HIIT exercise five times a week saw a dramatic temporary reduction in the function of their mitochondria, which provide energy production for most cells. Most fitness experts suggest no more than two 30-to-45-minute HIIT workouts per week.[1]

Body-weight HIIT workouts can be done in many locations and often take very little time.

performing body-weight HIIT exercises. That means that the body-weight HIIT exercises caused high levels of muscle fatigue. When those muscles recovered, that person had gained more powerful muscle from body-weight HIIT than from running sprints.

One of the main reasons body-weight HIIT is so accessible is that it takes very little time. The workout can be as short as 15 minutes, not including the warm-up and cooldown. "The results show that you can get an effective aerobic and strength workout at home, or wherever you happen to be, in less time than you might take for a coffee break," says fitness writer Gretchen Reynolds.[2]

The other key draw of body-weight HIIT workouts is how effective they can be at achieving personal fitness goals. Researchers in Australia noted that body-weight HIIT exercised many of the same muscle groups as

Circuit training often involves lunges. They can be done with or without weights. Variations, such as reverse lunges, involve different movement patterns.

a moderate intensity aerobics workout routine. The difference was that the HIIT workout took just less than half the time to complete.

CIRCUITS

There are numerous exercises that can make up a body-weight HIIT workout. They include well-known movements such as push-ups, lunges, and jumping jacks. Whatever movements are selected, they are done in what is called a circuit. A body-weight HIIT workout with six movements can be broken up in multiple ways. The simplest setup is to do each exercise once, with the proper amount of rest in between, until all six exercises have been completed. A person can then repeat that circuit as many times as they like.

Another way to set up a body-weight HIIT workout is by pairing two exercises together. Someone might start with a set of push-ups followed by a set of jumping jacks. They then repeat that sequence two more times, with rest after each set. Once they complete three reps of each, they move on to a new pair of exercises. This allows the muscles worked in the first movement to recover while a different set of muscles is worked out in the second movement.

There are many ways to adapt a body-weight HIIT workout. More experienced exercisers can crank the intensity up, perhaps by adding more exercises to a circuit or, alternately, more circuits. On the other hand, those who are just starting their fitness journey or recovering from injury or soreness can always change the amount or type of movements.

Exercisers can also change the length of both active periods as well as rest periods between body-weight movements. Those with more experience might take shorter breaks in between sets and between circuits, while others might need more time. A good starting point is to take a break of equal length to the work period. For example, a one-minute set might be followed by a one-minute break. From there, someone can adjust their

BURPEES FOR A CAUSE

In November 2023, the coaches at a gym in Maple Grove, Minnesota, challenged members of the community to donate money in honor of Veterans Day. The drive was called the 2,000 Burpees Challenge. For every dollar donated, the gym's employees would do one burpee. Each day's donation count was posted on the wall so the coaches knew how many burpees to do each day. The money went to charities for active and retired military service members.

rest time depending on their comfort level. "Something that's scalable is easier for people to utilize," says gym owner Jahkeen Washington.[3]

LUNGES

Lunges are basic movements that frequently appear in body-weight HIIT circuits. They strengthen your back, hips, and legs and can also improve balance, mobility, and leg stability. To perform a forward lunge, stand with your feet hip-width apart, then step forward with one leg. Make sure your feet stay hip-width apart, not directly in line with each other. Keep your back straight as you lower your hips until both of your knees are bent at a 90-degree angle. Then push off your front foot to return to the starting position. Repeat the movement by bringing your other leg forward.

Lunges can be done in numerous ways. The reverse lunge targets your core, glutes, and hamstrings. A walking lunge incorporates forward movement. Lateral lunges are done to the side, working both the inner and outer thighs. Other types of lunges include the curtsy lunge and the twist lunge.

BURPEES

The burpee is one of the most popular movements of a body-weight HIIT workout. The full-body move is also one of the most challenging. To begin a burpee, stand with your hands straight up above your head. Then drop down into a squat position and place your palms on the ground. From there, keep your hands on the ground and jump backward with both feet so that your body lands in a plank position. Perform a push-up, and then jump your feet back toward your hands in a squat. Rise up in

The burpee is named after Royal H. Burpee, who invented the technique as part of his doctoral thesis at Columbia University in the 1930s.

an explosive jump, reaching your hands back into the air. That sequence can be repeated for a set amount of time or repetitions (reps).

Burpees can be modified in ways that make them either easier or more challenging. If you need to back the intensity off, you can remove the push-up or the vertical leap elements or both. Holding on to a chair can also ease the transition from standing to the floor part of the exercise. If you want a bigger challenge, you can add a box jump instead of a simple vertical leap or hold on to a BOSU ball with the round part of the ball on the ground as you land in the plank position. That will test your ability to keep the ball stable as you do your push-up.

MOUNTAIN CLIMBERS

The mountain climber is an exercise designed to work the abdominal muscles and core. Start in a plank position. Then, take turns driving each knee forward toward your chest, as in a running motion. Engage your core to make sure you don't raise your hips too high or arch your lower back. Keep alternating for the set amount of time or reps before resting.

The main modification that can be made to a mountain climber set is the speed. Beginners might start slow, bringing each leg up deliberately. On the other hand, those looking for a challenge can turn the exercise

Mountain climbers can improve balance, agility, coordination, and blood circulation.

into a full sprint, bouncing off the balls of the feet to move quickly.

SQUATS

Squats are another common body-weight HIIT exercise. They work the quadriceps, glutes, and hip flexors. They are one of the more practical exercises because they mimic a motion used in everyday life. “When we perform squats, we use a movement pattern most of us are not only familiar with but use numerous times a day,” says trainer Sydney Bueckert.[4]

Start by standing with your feet shoulder-width apart and pointed forward. Then, inhale as you dip down and shift your hips back, making a sitting motion while keeping your chest up and your back straight. The goal

THE DREADED DOMS

One possible negative consequence of any HIIT workout is delayed onset muscle soreness (DOMS). It usually occurs when someone does an exercise their body is not ready for. This places an unnecessary load on a muscle. DOMS pain is usually first felt about 12 hours after a workout. But the highest intensity pain comes between 24 hours and 72 hours after the exercise.[6] Rest, ice, and medication are common treatments for anyone experiencing DOMS. However, the best way to avoid it is to progress through workouts at a steady pace, not increasing the intensity or weight until you know your body is ready.

of a squat is to bend the knees to a 90-degree angle, but do not bend your back in order to achieve that. Once you've gone as low as you can, drive back through your heels to rise up again.

Those looking for a more challenging movement can turn it into a squat jump. Squat jumps begin the same way, but as you rise, you leap straight into the air. Land on the balls of your feet with your knees soft, and immediately lower into a squat position again.

Squat jumps are a tiring part of any circuit. Fitness coaches often recommend they be performed near the beginning of a circuit before your legs get too fatigued from other exercises. They are also not recommended for beginners or those who are recovering from an injury. "[Squat jumps] are a high-impact exercise and would not aid in healing but could further the injury," says personal trainer Gina Newton.[5]

FITNESS SNAPSHOT

SQUAT

CHAPTER

HIIT WITH WEIGHTS

Adding weights to HIIT makes the exercises more difficult compared with body-weight training. However, with the added difficulty comes additional gain. By incorporating weights, a person can build strength in addition to HIIT's cardiovascular benefits.

Though the speed of the movements is generally the same in both cases, weighted HIIT is usually done by those who are more experienced. It is important to know proper weight-lifting form before adding weights to a HIIT workout. Poor technique is a major cause of injuries.

Most of the weights used in HIIT are free weights such as dumbbells and kettlebells. Some workouts will also use resistance bands. While this additional equipment comes at a cost, HIIT doesn't

Adding weights to a HIIT workout can up the intensity even more.

require a wide range of weights. Therefore, weighted HIIT workouts can still be done by those who do not have the time for or access to a gym. However, a gym will have barbells and weight lifting machines as well.

HYPERTROPHY

Adding weights changes the nature of HIIT workouts in many ways. Without added weight, the main ways to increase the intensity of an exercise are to up the speed, add more reps, or decrease rest intervals. All of those things are still possible when using weights, but it's also an option to simply add a heavier weight.

Another difference is that unweighted HIIT workouts involve movements that incorporate several muscle groups at once. This spreads out the focus of each exercise. Weighted exercises usually involve movements that target specific muscles.

ADJUSTABLE WEIGHTS

Many companies sell adjustable weights, which take up much less space than a set of dumbbells with several different weights. Rather than requiring a new dumbbell for each exercise, an adjustable set has several different weights all connected together. All it takes to add or remove weight is adjusting a dial or pressing a button. These sets make home workout equipment much more compact, but adjustable weights aren't always cheap. Sets may cost anywhere from $300 to nearly $800.[1]

Body-weight exercises are a good way to ease into a weighted HIIT workout.

By adding weight and targeting specific muscles, exercisers are aiming for what is called hypertrophy. The term refers to the increase in muscle size. Hypertrophy is caused partly by microscopic breakdowns, known as microtears, in the muscles when they are exerted.

The microtears cause an inflammatory response in the muscles, so with rest and proper nutrition, the same muscles build back up stronger. The process of microtearing activates structures in the skeletal cells that increase the amount of protein in the muscle. This allows someone to increase weight for the next workout and begin this process again.

APPS AND VIDEOS

Technology offers many ways to find and perform HIIT workouts. Apps can be downloaded that offer HIIT classes. Some charge a fee. One of these is Nike Training Club, which includes HIIT, yoga, and other types of workouts, along with tips on nutrition and recovery.

Another is Keelo, which focuses solely on HIIT. It lets users build workouts from more than 180 unique exercises, and it also tracks their workout history. The Apple Fitness+ service features regularly updated workout videos hosted by experienced trainers. It also integrates with the company's Apple Watch to track heart rate during HIIT sessions.

There are also free HIIT videos available online, including through YouTube. People can search for videos focusing on body-weight routines, dumbbells, gym equipment, and more. Some videos feature countdown clocks during each interval period to help viewers

Virtual workout classes offer the chance to do HIIT workouts at home or while traveling.

track each part of the workout. They sometimes include a preview video window that shows which exercise is up next. Many include motivational music in the background.

Apps and videos both offer workouts for various skill levels. So wherever the person is in their workout journey, they can find something that challenges them. These technology tools make HIIT accessible to anyone. However, exercise physiologist Pete McCall suggests making educated decisions before downloading an app. "Use them as a learning tool," McCall says. "They'll give you some great circuit ideas, and you can always make adjustments that work for you as you get more comfortable."[2]

Choosing light weights is the best way to avoid overtraining during a HIIT workout.

WARMING UP

It is important to engage in a proper warm-up before beginning a weighted HIIT workout. Many people choose to do basic body-weight exercises and stretches as a warm-up. Because these exercises are low impact, they are a good way to ease into more strenuous workout activity.

A typical warm-up might include an interval of jumping jacks. That can be followed by an interval of arm circles, high knees, lunges, or body-weight squats. There is no set length for an effective warm-up. But it is important to feel nimble and loose before adding weights to a workout.

PICK A STRUCTURE

How you incorporate weights into a HIIT workout depends on your experience level. If you are new to this type of exercise, it is important to set up a plan that includes the right resistance. One way to do this is by choosing light weights. Another is to choose either shorter work periods or longer periods of rest.

A simple weight lifting HIIT routine might include 30 seconds of weighted squats followed by 30 seconds of rest. This can then be repeated with 30 seconds of another exercise, such as a bench press, barbell dead lift, dumbbell or barbell row, and overhead press using dumbbells. This can be repeated as many times as you are comfortable. However, it is important not to overtrain. While HIIT sets generally consist of more repetitions of lighter weights, doing too much can lead to excessive muscle soreness or injury.

BENCH PRESS

The bench press is one of the most common weight workouts. While it is usually associated with power lifters, it can also be an effective HIIT workout. It is often seen as a weighted replacement for push-ups, as the two exercises work similar muscles. Generally, when bench pressing as part of a HIIT workout, it is better to choose a slightly lower weight than you could normally lift. This will help offset the speed and intensity of HIIT lifting.

A bench press can be done with either a barbell or dumbbells. Lie on a workout bench or the floor with your feet flat on the floor. Hold the barbell or dumbbells above your chest with your arms straight. Lock your core as you bend your elbows to lower the weight toward your chest. Make sure your bent arms are at about a 45-degree angle from your shoulders. Exhale as you push the weight back up. Pause briefly once you have extended your arms again.

There are many ways to modify a bench press. In addition to adjusting the weight and intensity of the lift, you can change your grip when working on a bar, adjusting everything from the width between your hands to how they are positioned. Most workout benches are also adjustable, allowing you to position the bench at different angles. These angles work different parts of the body.

DUMBBELL MOVEMENTS

Many people choose to stick with dumbbells for weighted HIIT exercises. They are much easier to store at home than larger weight equipment, which makes them

Bench press exercises can be done with a barbell or with free weights.

FITNESS SNAPSHOT

RENEGADE ROW

Keep shoulder blades down and back and spine neutral

Pull dumbbell up to ribs by squeezing shoulder blades toward spine

Use core, legs, and opposite arm for balance

Place feet hip-width apart

Start in push-up position, with hands on dumbbells and palms facing each other that might require a change of hand position. For these reasons, kettlebells are a popular tool in HIIT workouts.

One of the most common kettlebell movements is a kettlebell swing. To perform a swing, stand with your legs slightly wider than shoulder-width apart. Hold the flat part of the handle in both hands. Hinge your hips backward and lower the kettlebell down between your legs.

Once you feel a stretch in your hamstrings, squeeze your glutes and drive your hips forward to come back to standing. Your arms should not rise higher than shoulder level. Hinge again and bring the kettlebell back down between your legs as it falls. Repeat as needed to complete a set.

A single-arm shoulder press is another movement easily done with a kettlebell. Stand tall with your feet hip-width apart. It's important throughout to keep your core tight. Before each rep, the kettlebell is held in what is called the front rack position.

KETTLEBELL HISTORY

Kettlebells were originally used in the 1700s in Russia to weigh crops and goods. However, the country's military found that they were an effective exercise tool and began using them to train soldiers. By the late 1800s, kettlebell lifting competitions had become popular in Russia. One competitor, Pyotr Krylov, was nicknamed the King of Kettlebells for his amazing feats of strength. He once lifted a 227-pound (103 kg) dumbbell using only his pinkie finger.[4]

Despite how it looks, the kettlebell swing is powered by the glutes and hamstrings.

To get into the front rack position, hold the handle with one hand in an overhand grip. Keep your elbow close to your side and bend it until your forearm is mostly vertical and is close to your chest. Your hand is at collar bone level, and your thumb faces you. The ball part of the kettlebell should comfortably rest on your forearm, biceps, and chest muscles. Make sure your wrist stays straight as well.

Slowly press the kettlebell straight up until your arm is fully extended above your shoulder. As you press, make sure your shoulder stays down and away from your ears, and rotate your wrist slightly so your palm is facing forward at the top. Carefully lower the kettlebell to return to the front rack position. Complete a set on one side, then repeat the movement with your other arm.

HIIT IN MOTION

While body-weight and HIIT with weights workouts have clear benefits, many people opt for HIIT workouts based on movement. Running, biking, swimming, rowing, and even walking can be adapted into HIIT workouts. In all cases, people can see gains in their cardiovascular fitness and even increased speed.

One key difference between movement-based HIIT workouts and others is in the name itself—movement. While body-weight and weight exercises often mix moves with rest, movement workouts often proceed without stopping. Instead, they are separated into segments of faster and slower movement.

With all movement workouts it is important to have a proper meal two to three hours beforehand.

Swimmers can easily adapt HIIT workouts for their needs.

SKATING IN THE DARK

One of the most unique HIIT movement workouts ever done came as a punishment. In the buildup to the 1980 Winter Olympics in Lake Placid, New York, the United States men's hockey team played an exhibition game in Norway. The game ended in a tie, infuriating the team's stern head coach, Herb Brooks. He forced the team to stay on the ice, where they skated sprints up and down the rink for nearly 45 minutes. The rink manager even turned the lights off in the building, hoping it would clear the players out, but Brooks kept his exhausted team skating in the dark. Brooks's extremely fit group went on to win gold at the Games.

Working out at intense levels on an empty stomach can cause dizziness and fatigue. Because of this, it is important to stay hydrated both before and during exercise. Keep a water bottle with you while you work out. It is wise to take small sips during the slower recovery phases of the exercises.

WALKING

It might be hard to imagine getting your heart rate up high enough to qualify as high intensity simply through walking, but it is possible. Many walking HIIT workouts require a treadmill. That way you can control the speed and the incline. Walking workouts are a low-risk way to incorporate HIIT, which makes them ideal for beginners. "An interval walking program can boost the intensity and calorie burn without adding too much stress or strain to your body," writes health coach Malia Frey.[1]

An effective HIIT workout with movement can be as simple as mixing walking speeds.

Incorporating stairs into a HIIT running workout can provide an even greater challenge.

Different workouts use different strategies to achieve the same effect. One possibility is to break a walking workout on a treadmill into blocks. In each block, slowly increase the intensity. Start by walking at a moderate speed. Then, over the course of a set time period, slowly increase the incline. Eventually, you should be walking on the steepest setting you are comfortable with.

Once you have completed a minute at the steepest incline, bring the ramp all the way back down to start a new workout segment. In each segment that follows, use less time to ramp the incline fully back up. You might take only five minutes to reach the highest incline setting during the second segment and only three minutes in the third.

Make sure to adjust the speed of the treadmill accordingly as you increase the incline. Walking at a high speed on a high incline at the same time can be dangerous. Keep at a manageable speed throughout to keep yourself safe.

RUNNING

HIIT running workouts feature periods of sprinting alternated with slower segments. These intervals may involve slower movements, such as jogging or walking. They may also involve stopping completely to rest.

As with walking workouts, you can customize a running workout in many ways. One option is to start with a light warm-up for two to three minutes. Then, while keeping track of your distance on a treadmill or wearable fitness device, do five sets of 500-foot (150 m) sprints. Between each set, either rest or slow to a walking pace. After those are completed, do another set of five 300-foot (90 m) sprints, interrupting each with a slower pace or rest. When the main exercise is complete, be sure to cool down and stretch.

BIKING

Biking is another exercise that can be performed as HIIT. It can be done indoors on a stationary bicycle or outdoors on a road or bike path. Overall, biking is a low-impact exercise. It is a good choice for those with joint issues. Riders can also experience an added feeling of well-being because of the sunlight, fresh air, and beautiful views of nature.

Fitness writer Sara Lindberg offers two outdoor biking HIIT routines. The first uses a moderately inclined hill. She says to warm up for ten minutes at an easy pace. Then, intensely cycle up the moderate hill for one minute. Turn around and ride down the hill at an easier pace. Alternate these rounds ten times. Follow up with a cooldown period of easy biking for ten minutes.[2]

Lindberg's second workout can be done on a flat road that has little car traffic. She says to warm up for 15 minutes at a moderate pace. Then, alternate between two minutes of intense biking and four minutes of moderate recovery riding. Repeat this for 50 minutes. Finish with a 15-minute cooldown at moderate effort.[3]

A stationary bike HIIT routine is similar to those outlined for outdoors. Lindberg describes a workout that begins

CHOOSING A BIKE

A person needs to choose an outdoor bicycle suited for where they plan to ride. Mountain bikes have wide, knobby tires that perform well on bumpy dirt trails. Road bikes, with thinner and smoother tires, are good for paved roads. Road bikes usually have handlebars that curve down. A hybrid bike is a mixture of the two styles and can travel easily on the road and off.

Biking HIIT workouts can incorporate sprints on flat surfaces or use hills to increase the difficulty.

with a five-minute warm-up. Stationary bikes allow the rider to control the resistance level, so the challenge of the intense and moderate sections of the workout can be modified depending on your fitness level and preference. Riders alternate between a one-minute work period and two-minute recovery for a block of 15 minutes. The workout ends with a five-minute cooldown at an easy pace.[4]

ROWING

Rowing is a full-body workout that can engage up to 90 percent of the body's muscles at one time.[5]

FITNESS SNAPSHOT

ROWING TECHNIQUE

Keep head and neck straight

Begin pulling with arms just before legs straighten

Avoid locking knees when legs straighten

Keep bar parallel to the floor and pull it

Start by pushing from the legs

Like running and walking, it can be done at a slow, steady pace as an aerobic activity, or it can be incorporated into a HIIT workout for greater anaerobic benefits. Most people who row outdoors do so as a competitive sport, but it can be done as exercise with a rowing shell or small boat. However, most rowing for exercise is done indoors on a dedicated rowing machine.

One advantage rowing has over running is that it is a lower-impact exercise, which can save wear and tear on the knee and ankle joints. However, it is important to practice proper form when rowing. Despite its low-impact nature, rowing incorrectly can cause injury to the wrists, back, and biceps. Keeping workouts short, especially at the start, is also advised. "I recommend beginners keep HIIT rowing workouts to 15 minutes or less, and start with just one per week, working up to three over the course of several weeks," says fitness writer Amanda Capritto.[6]

All rowing workouts should start with a warm-up. How long the warm-up lasts often depends on the total length of your workout. However, you should plan to spend the first two to five minutes rowing at a steady, moderate pace to warm up your body and loosen your joints.

Once the workout begins, there are many options. One is a pyramid workout, which starts with shorter periods of intense activity and slowly builds up to longer sets. Each segment is broken up by a period of either rest

ROCK CLIMBING

Rock climbing is a popular sport. Some people rock climb in indoor climbing gyms. Others do rock climbing outdoors. Either way, HIIT can help a rock climber get into top shape. In his book *The Rock Climber's Exercise Guide,* Eric Hörst suggests using HIIT as a preparation for rock climbing. He does HIIT while running on a track. He says to start with a warm-up, then run at a fast pace for half a lap and walk or jog for half a lap. Do this for a total of 15 to 30 minutes.[7] Finally, do a cooldown. HIIT gets the rock climber's body ready to switch between the difficult parts of the route and the less challenging portions.

or moderate rowing. After reaching the peak time, slowly shorten the periods of high intensity until you are back down to the original length.

Another possibility is the 10-20-30 workout. Start with a five-minute warm-up at moderate intensity. Begin the work period by rowing slowly for 30 seconds. Without resting, speed up your rowing to moderate intensity for the next 20 seconds. Follow that up with ten seconds of maximum intensity. This completes one cycle.

Repeat this cycle three or four times. Rest for two minutes before starting the next batch of cycles. Cool down with another five-minute period of moderate rowing, followed by stretching.

SWIMMING

Swimming is a highly beneficial form of exercise. It's aerobic, so it brings oxygen into the body by working the heart and lungs. It is also low impact. Unlike exercises such as running or dancing, the weight of the water supports a person's body. This resistance also helps tone muscles.

Swimming is also good exercise for those with joint problems, such as arthritis. A person with arthritis might have pain if they perform weight-bearing exercises, but swimming is easier on the joints. For the same reason, someone with back trouble might face less chance of injury while swimming than with a weight-bearing exercise.

Swimmers do laps in lanes that cross the pool's length. They swim using strokes including the front crawl, breaststroke, backstroke, and butterfly. For the best full-body workout, it is good to switch between strokes during the workout period. You should wait two hours after a large meal to swim. This will help avoid cramps.

Swimming can be adapted into a HIIT workout by varying high-intensity swimming with gentler movement. For example, you might perform five minutes of intense swimming followed by five minutes of recovery. This can be adjusted depending on your fitness level and exercise goals.

MIXING IT UP

HIIT workouts are noted for their customizable nature. In the same way you can mix body-weight and weight-based

HIIT workouts, you can also combine either of those with movement-based workouts. As long as you have the right equipment, HIIT possibilities are vast.

One easy way to combine exercises is to move between running on a treadmill and doing body-weight training exercises. Start with a set of 500-foot (150 m) sprints, then move off the treadmill and mix in eight sets of squats, squat jumps, and planks. Other movements can be added or used to customize the workout however you like. Once you have completed those sets, hop back on the treadmill and complete five sets of 300-foot (90 m) sprints.

Many treadmills or elliptical machines have built-in HIIT workout settings.

CHAPTER

TABATA

While HIIT workouts are known for their vigorous levels of exertion, one form of HIIT takes this to the extreme. The active period of a Tabata workout is 20 seconds. Each is followed by a ten-second rest. Because it is done in such an efficient way, it is also known for being incredibly demanding.

That cycle of 20 seconds on and ten seconds off repeats for four minutes. While it sounds like short bursts are simple, the idea behind Tabata is that the repetition of these short, intense sequences adds up to a tough workout. "These are going to feel like very long minutes," says exercise physiologist Katie Lawton. "There is a lot of effort packed into a short time—and you're going to feel it."[1]

Tabata workouts use the same movements as other HIIT workouts, only at a higher intensity.

MAKING A CHAMPION

One of the athletes Izumi Tabata worked with in the 1990s was speed skater Hiroyasu Shimizu. At the 1998 Winter Games, Shimizu won the gold medal in the 500 meters and the bronze medal in the 1000 meters. His gold was the first Japan had ever won in speed skating.

HISTORY OF TABATA

In the 1990s, Izumi Tabata was a doctor who worked with the Japanese Olympic speed skating team. One of his tasks was analyzing the team's performance leading up to the 1998 Winter Games, which were held in Nagano, Japan. He decided to run a study. He had one group of skaters do moderate level workouts five times per week over a six-week stretch. Then he told a second group to try four-minute workouts just four days per week for the same period.

Tabata found that the second group improved not only their cardiovascular fitness but also their muscular performance. Those workouts became the basis of Tabata. The trend grew around the world and is now one of the most popular HIIT workouts available.

EFFICIENCY AND DISCIPLINE

Tabata is a quick exercise routine. A full Tabata workout takes only 20 minutes. It is made of four exercises done for four minutes each. Every set is followed by a one-minute break.

The key to a Tabata workout is also what sets it apart from other HIIT routines. While the exercise-versus-rest ratio can be adjusted for any other routine, it cannot for a Tabata routine. The intervals of 20 seconds exercise and ten seconds of rest are nonnegotiable.

The other key to Tabata is the level at which each exercise is carried out. Tabata calls for maximum effort for

Researchers have discovered that Tabata can burn more than 13 calories per minute.

THE IRISAWA WORKOUT?

While Izumi Tabata is credited with inventing the exercise named after him, he doesn't claim to own the idea. He says that the Japanese speed skating coach Kouichi Irisawa was already training his athletes with the method, and Irisawa merely asked Tabata to study its effectiveness. In an interview Tabata joked, "Although Coach Irisawa pioneered the idea, somehow it became named after me."[4]

20 seconds. If that effort sags even a little, Tabata is not as effective. But Izumi Tabata himself doesn't know exactly how far the effectiveness drops if the intensity lowers. He continued studying the effects of the Tabata workouts into the 2020s. But those who swear by Tabata are certain that all-out effort matters. "If you're not absolutely toast after those four minutes, you didn't go hard enough," says fitness expert Obi Obadike.[2]

One way to keep a full effort through an entire Tabata workout is to count your reps. That will give you a baseline goal to reach in the next 20-second interval. If you did seven squat jumps in one work period, try to match that total or beat it in the next round.

This will naturally become more difficult as fatigue sets in over the course of the workout, but it will help maintain focus. It will also help you see progress over the course of weeks and months as you repeat Tabata exercises. Lawton says, "the goal is to set the bar high and then meet it again and again."[3]

Tabata routines are not as adaptable as regular HIIT workouts since the ratio of work to rest is much stricter.

TABATA MOVEMENTS

There are no set movements that make up a Tabata workout. Like most forms of HIIT, the individual exercises can be customized. The exercises themselves are all regular HIIT exercises. Popular exercises for Tabata include burpees, crunches, high knees, mountain climbers, push-ups, and squat jumps.

One popular move comes from speed skating. The skate lunge works your core, glutes, hamstrings, and thighs in addition to providing a cardiovascular workout. Start by standing wide. Lift one leg slightly off the ground and place it behind your standing leg. Bend slightly forward, keeping your back flat and your core tight.

Once you have your balance, hop sideways so that you land on your other foot. At the same time, swing your arms so that the opposite arm from your landing foot swings in front of your body. Move your free leg behind your standing leg. Repeat that motion back and forth for the rest of the interval.

MODIFYING TABATA

Tabata is not limited to body-weight exercises. Experts say that weights and machines can be used in a Tabata workout. Kettlebells can be added to many movements, such as squats. Medicine balls are frequently used during

FITNESS SNAPSHOT

SKATE LUNGE

Swing arms to keep opposite arm in front of body

Keep core tight and back flat

Bend knee of standing leg

Bring opposite leg behind standing leg and tap toes on ground

Hop sideways, pushing off from one leg and landing on the other

Tabata can be done with equipment, but exercisers must stick to the strict timing rules it requires.

Tabata workout circuits for movements such as tosses and twists.

The original speed skaters who tested Tabata used stationary bikes. Rowing machines are also useful for a Tabata workout. However, experts warn against using treadmills in Tabata workouts. Because they take time to get up to speed, it is difficult to hit the precise 20-second intervals required.

TABATA IN THE POOL

Tabata can be a swimming exercise as well. Health researcher Nikki Lyn Pugh suggests that the circuits can be made of 20 seconds of full-speed freestyle swimming, followed by ten seconds of back floating.[5] That can be repeated eight times for a full Tabata circuit.

ESSENTIAL FACTS

What Is High-Intensity Interval Training?

- High-intensity interval training (HIIT) is an exercise routine that alternates vigorous exercise periods with low- to moderate-intensity periods.
- The goal is to approach maximum heart rate during the high-intensity work periods, then lower the heart rate during the moderate-intensity recovery periods.
- HIIT can involve cardiovascular exercise, body-weight movements, or weights.
- Tabata is an advanced form of HIIT named after Japanese speed skating coach Izumi Tabata. Work periods are strictly 20 seconds, and recovery periods are ten seconds of rest.

Benefits of High-Intensity Interval Training

- Keeps the heart, blood vessels, and lungs healthy.
- Strengthens muscles and bones.
- Improves mental health, including reduced symptoms of depression and anxiety.
- Provides an effective workout in less time.
- Allows a person to customize a workout that they will enjoy.

Quote

"The main advantage to HIIT is that you can boost your cardiovascular fitness faster by working harder instead of longer."

—Julie Corliss,
medical writer

GLOSSARY

accountable
Responsible.

alternate
To change between two things repeatedly.

biceps
The large muscle on the front of the upper arm between the elbow and shoulder.

bone density
The mass of a person's bones, which indicates bone strength.

BOSU ball
An exercise tool with a rubbery inflated dome on one side and a flat platform on the other.

chronic
Continuing or occurring repeatedly for a long time.

cognitive function
Mental abilities that include learning, thinking, reasoning, memory, problem solving, decision making, and attention.

continuous
Uninterrupted.

customize
To change to meet a specific need or desire.

dead lift

A weight-lifting move that brings a weight from the floor to hip level by standing.

forehand

A tennis stroke that is played on the same side of the body on which the racket is held.

moderate

Of a medium amount.

rep

Short for repetition, a single execution of an exercise, such as one push-up.

resistance

An opposing force a person uses to exercise muscles to increase muscle strength.

sedentary

Not physically active or exercising regularly.

sprain

A tearing of a ligament, which attaches bones together.

technique

A form or method of carrying out a task.

ADDITIONAL RESOURCES

Selected Bibliography

"HIIT (High Intensity Interval Training)." *Harvard T. H. Chan School of Public Health*, 2003, hsph.harvard.edu. Accessed 13 Nov. 2023.

Kravitz, Len. *HIIT Your Limit: High-Intensity Interval Training for Fat Loss, Cardio, and Full Body Health*. Apollo, 2018.

Mayo Clinic. "How High-Intensity Intervals Impact Cardiovascular Health." *Mayo Clinic*, 12 Jan. 2022, mcpress.mayoclinic.org. Accessed 13 Nov. 2023.

Further Readings

Clay, Ingrid S. *Science of HIIT: High-Intensity Interval Training: Understand the Anatomy and Physiology to Transform Your Body*. DK, 2022.

Kelley, Roosevelt, *HIIT: Everything You Need to Know About High Intensity Interval Training*. Jennifer Windy, 2021.

Scirri, Kaitlin. *Aerobic Exercise*. Abdo, 2025.

Online Resources

To learn more about high-intensity interval training, please visit **abdobooklinks.com** or scan this QR code. These links are routinely monitored and updated to provide the most current information available.

More Information

For more information on this subject, contact or visit the following organizations:

American College of Sports Medicine (ACSM)

401 W. Michigan St.
Indianapolis, IN 46202
acsm.org

The ACSM represents 70 sports medicine professions. Its mission is to offer educational and practical applications for exercise science and sports medicine. The ACSM offers a number of materials related to HIIT, including workout materials and links to scientific studies.

National Academy of Sports Medicine (NASM)

355 Germann Rd., Ste. 201
Gilbert, AZ 85297
nasm.org

The NASM promotes initiatives related to sports medicine, fitness, and personal training. The organization offers certifications in fitness teaching and coaching, including for those seeking to offer HIIT classes.

National Exercise Trainers Association

12800 Industrial Park Blvd.
Minneapolis, MN 55411
netafit.org

The National Exercise Trainers Association trains exercise professionals and promotes fitness initiatives. The organization's website includes several HIIT-related books and online learning materials.

SOURCE NOTES

Chapter 1. Hitting a Wall

1. Jacky Anderson. "Interval Training for Sport Specific Endurance." *Sport Fitness Advisor*, n.d., sport-fitness-advisor.com. Accessed 10 Mar. 2024.

2. Amanda Capritto and Giselle Castro-Sloboda. "Here's How to Determine What Time of Day You Should Exercise." *CNET*, 4 Feb. 2024, cnet.com. Accessed 20 Feb. 2024.

Chapter 2. What Is High-Intensity Interval Training?

1. "Tips for Monitoring Aerobic Exercise Intensity." *American College of Sports Medicine*, n.d., acsm.org. Accessed 20 Feb. 2024.

2. Len Kravitz. *HIIT Your Limit: High-Intensity Interval Training for Fat Loss, Cardio, and Full Body Health*. Apollo, 2018. 19.

3. Pantelis T. Nikolaidis, et al. "Age-Predicted Maximal Heart Rate in Recreational Marathon Runners: A Cross-Sectional Study on Fox's and Tanaka's Equations." *Frontiers in Physiology*, vol. 9, no. 15, Mar. 2018, pubmed.ncbi.nlm.nih.gov. Accessed 20 Feb. 2024.

4. "Age-Predicted Maximal Heart Rate."

5. "How to Take Your Wrist Pulse." *Medline Plus*, n.d., medlineplus.com. Accessed 20 Feb. 2024.

6. "Perceived Exertion (Borg Rating of Perceived Exertion Scale)." *United States Centers for Disease Control and Prevention*, n.d., cdc.gov. Accessed 20 Feb. 2024.

Chapter 3. High-Intensity Interval Training and the Body

1. Julie Corliss. "High-Intensity Exercise and Your Heart." *Harvard Health Publishing*, 1 Dec. 2021, health.harvard.edu. Accessed 20 Feb. 2024.

2. Amanda MacMillan. "Researchers Have Found Yet Another Benefit of HIIT Workouts." *Sports Illustrated*, 10 Mar. 2017, si.com. Accessed 20 Feb. 2024.

3. "Cancer Stat Facts: Cancer of Any Site." *National Cancer Institute*, n.d., seer.cancer.gov. Accessed 20 Feb. 2024.

4. Michelle Blowes. "Short Bursts of Daily Activity Linked to Reduced Cancer Risk." *University of Sydney*, 28 Jul. 2023, sydney.edu.au. Accessed 20 Feb. 2024.

5. "Short Bursts of Daily Activity Linked to Reduced Cancer Risk."

6. Beth JoJack. "Metastatic Cancer Risk Reduced by as Much as 72% with High Intensity Exercise." *Medical News Today*, 18 Nov. 2022, medicalnewstoday.com. Accessed 20 Feb. 2024.

7. Jens Plag, et al. "Working Out the Worries: A Randomized Controlled Trial of High Intensity Interval Training in Generalized Anxiety Disorder." *Journal of Anxiety Disorders*, vol. 76, Dec. 2020, sciencedirect.com. Accessed 20 Feb. 2024.

SOURCE NOTES CONTINUED

Chapter 4. Body-Weight HIIT

1. Gretchen Reynolds. "Too Much High-Intensity Exercise May Be Bad for Your Health." *New York Times*, 10 Nov. 2021, nytimes.com. Accessed 20 Feb. 2024.

2. Gretchen Reynolds. "The Speedy Scientific Workout You Can Do Almost Anywhere." *Washington Post*, 4 Nov. 2022, washingtonpost.com. Accessed 20 Feb. 2024.

3. Mitch Calvert and Cori Ritchey. "These HIIT Workouts Will Make You Forget Boring Cardio." *Men's Health*, 31 Oct. 2023, menshealth.com. Accessed 20 Feb. 2024.

4. Sydney Bueckert. "Bodyweight Squats: Benefits, Form, and How the Row-N-Ride® Can Help." *Sunny Health & Fitness*, 22 Oct. 2021, sunnyhealthfitness.com. Accessed 20 Feb. 2024.

5. Dina Cheney. "Everything You Need to Know about Jump Squats." *Nike*, 24 Oct. 2022, nike.com. Accessed 20 Feb. 2024.

6. "Delayed Onset Muscle Soreness (DOMS)." *American College of Sports Medicine*, n.d., acsm.org. Accessed 20 Feb. 2024.

Chapter 5. HIIT with Weights

1. Seth Berkman and Ingrid Skjong. "The Best Adjustable Dumbbells." *New York Times*, 4 Dec. 2023, nytimes.com. Accessed 20 Feb. 2024.

2. Ashley Mateo. "5 HIIT Workout Apps You Should Download Now." *Shape*, 8 July, 2022, shape.com. Accessed 14 Mar. 2024.

3. Jeff Tomko. "This Hellish 5-Minute Workout Will Get You Ready for the NFL Combine." *Men's Health*, 28 Feb. 2023, menshealth.com. Accessed 20 Feb. 2024.

4. "Pyotr Kryloff." *Legendary Strength*, 28 Mar. 2014, legendarystrength.com. Accessed 20 Feb. 2024.

Chapter 6. HIIT in Motion

1. Malia Frey. "How to Use Interval Walking for Weight Loss." *Verywell Fit*, 3 Aug. 2022, verywellfit.com. Accessed 20 Feb. 2024.

2. Sara Lindberg. "2 Outdoor Cycling HIIT Workouts for Lower-Body Endurance." *Livestrong*, 8 Oct. 2019, livestrong.com. Accessed 20 Feb. 2024.

3. "Outdoor Cycling HIIT Workouts."

4. Sara Lindberg. "How to Do Indoor Cycling HIIT Workouts—And a 25-Minute Routine to Try." *Livestrong*, 31 Mar. 2020, livestrong.com. Accessed 20 Feb. 2024.

5. "4 Reasons to Add a Rower to Your Fitness Space." *Core Health & Fitness*, n.d., corehandf.com. Accessed 20 Feb. 2024.

6. Lindsay Boyers. "Send Your Heart Rate Soaring with a HIIT Rowing Workout." *Garage Gym Reviews*, 20 Sept. 2023, garagegymreviews.com. Accessed 20 Feb. 2024.

7. Eric J. Hörst. *The Rock Climber's Exercise Guide*. FalconGuides, 2017. 188–189.

Chapter 7. Tabata

1. "Tabata vs. HIIT: What's the Difference?" *Cleveland Clinic*, 7 Jul. 2021, health.clevelandclinic.org. Accessed 20 Feb. 2024.

2. Nikki Lyn Pugh. "What Is Tabata and Why Is It So Popular?" *Organixx*, 29 Apr. 2022, organixx.com. Accessed 20 Feb. 2024.

3. "Tabata vs. HIIT"

4. "Featured Researchers: Professor Izumi Tabata." *Ritsumeikan University*, n.d., ritsumei.ac.jp. Accessed 20 Feb. 2024.

5. "What Is Tabata?"

INDEX

ABOUT THE AUTHOR

Marie-Therese Miller

Marie-Therese Miller is an award-winning author of more than 35 nonfiction books for children and teens. Her recent selections include *Sly as a Fox: Are Foxes Clever?, A Dog's Best Friend: A Sesame Street Guide to Caring for Your Dog, Being Thankful with Gabrielle: A Book About Gratitude,* and *Esports Superstars*. Miller earned her PhD in English from St. John's University, with an academic focus on James Thurber's humorous writing. She teaches Children's and YA Literature at Marist College. Miller and her husband have five grown children and a grandson.